PUFFIN BOOKS

Unicorn School

Team Magic

Willow glanced up just as the Tricorn looked
around at them all, his eyes concentrating
particularly on the Year Ones. 'I will *not* have
cheating in this school,' he said firmly.
'We will find out who did this. If it is you, I urge
you to come forward before it is too late.'

Linda Chapman lives in Leicestershire with her family and Bernese mountain dogs. She used to be a stage manager in the theatre. When she is not writing she spends her time looking after her young family, horse riding and teaching drama. You can find out more about Linda on her website *lindachapman.co.uk* or visit *mysecretunicorn.co.uk*

Unicorn School

Team Magic

Linda Chapman

Illustrated by Ann Kronheimer

PUFFIN

PUFFIN BOOKS

Published by the Penguin Group
Penguin Books Ltd, 80 Strand, London WC2R 0RL, England
Penguin Group (USA) Inc., 375 Hudson Street, New York, New York 10014, USA
Penguin Group (Canada), 90 Eglinton Avenue East, Suite 700, Toronto, Ontario, Canada M4P 2Y3
(a division of Pearson Penguin Canada Inc.)
Penguin Ireland, 25 St Stephen's Green, Dublin 2, Ireland (a division of Penguin Books Ltd)
Penguin Group (Australia), 250 Camberwell Road, Camberwell, Victoria 3124, Australia
(a division of Pearson Australia Group Pty Ltd)
Penguin Books India Pvt Ltd, 11 Community Centre, Panchsheel Park, New Delhi – 110 017, India
Penguin Group (NZ), 67 Apollo Drive, Rosedale, North Shore 0632, New Zealand
(a division of Pearson New Zealand Ltd)
Penguin Books (South Africa) (Pty) Ltd, 24 Sturdee Avenue, Rosebank, Johannesburg 2196, South Africa

Penguin Books Ltd, Registered Offices: 80 Strand, London WC2R 0RL, England

puffinbooks.com

First published 2009

I

Text copyright © Working Partners Ltd 2009
Illustrations copyright © Ann Kronheimer, 2009
All rights reserved

The moral right of the author and illustrator has been asserted

Set in Bembo
Typeset by Palimpsest Book Production Ltd, Grangemouth, Stirlingshire
Made and printed in England by Clays Ltd, St Ives plc

British Library Cataloguing in Publication Data
A CIP catalogue record for this book is available from the British Library

ISBN: 978-0-141-32252-0

To Suzanne Duxbury, for all the friendship, help and support — and for going through everything with me!

Contents

Delivering the Mail

The sun shone down on the glittering, pearly-white turrets of Unicorn School. It was early in the morning and most of the unicorns were still in their stables. Willow trotted across the courtyard, a mailbag swinging from her mouth. She felt very important. Usually all the letters and parcels that came to Unicorn School were delivered by the elves who worked there, but that morning Willow had got up early to post a birthday card to her dad and had been asked to help. It was very exciting to be getting mail because the end-of-year exams were coming up and all the parents kept sending good-luck cards and little presents.

As Willow thought about the exams, a nervous shiver ran down her spine. She was in her first year at Unicorn School, which meant she had six exams to take, and she really wanted to do well. She'd been working very hard every evening for the last few weeks, reading through all her notes for the year. There was so much to remember!

She trotted into the tower that led up to the Rainbow House stables. All of the unicorns who went to Unicorn School belonged to one of four houses, the others being Star

House, Moon House and Sun House. Willow slept and ate with the seven other Year Ones who were also in Rainbow House. At the very top of the tower there was a circular room with a door in the wall that led into the stables, set in the clouds.

Carrying the mailbag carefully, Willow went across the room and touched the door with her silver horn. The door swung open, revealing a corridor leading into a stable with eight stalls. Two of Willow's best friends, Sapphire and Storm, had their heads over their stall doors and were chatting.

'Hi, Willow!' Storm whinnied as she came down the corridor. He looked at the bag. 'What have you got there?'

'*Mwmph*,' Willow mumbled through a mouthful of bag. She put it down carefully. 'Mail!' she said. 'The elves are really busy with all the post that keeps arriving so they asked me if I would deliver it.' She opened the bag and started to give out the packages and letters. 'There's a parcel for you, Sapphire.' She passed a pink parcel to a very pretty unicorn with long eyelashes and a sweeping mane and tail. 'And this is for you, Storm.' She handed the tall unicorn a yellow parcel. 'This green parcel is for Flint, the orange one for Starlight, and then there are letters for Topaz and Ash.' She trotted between the stalls giving out the mail to the other Year Ones. They all whinnied gratefully.

'Is there anything for me?' asked a voice behind her.

Willow looked round. It was Troy, her other best friend. From his windswept mane and tail she guessed that he had been out at early morning practice with the Flying Team.

'There's a letter for you,' said Willow. 'It looks like it's from your mum and dad,' she added, seeing that it had a gold crown on the front. Troy's parents were the King and Queen of Arcadia.

'Oh, good!' said Troy, pleased. 'I

wrote to Mum asking her about
something important. I bet she's
replying to that.'

'What were you asking about?'
Willow said curiously.

Troy shook his head. 'I'm not telling.'

'Why not?' asked Willow.

'Because it's something about you three,' said Troy, looking at Storm and Sapphire.

'About us?' Storm said in surprise.

'What is it?' whinnied Sapphire.

'I said I'm not telling,' said Troy mysteriously. 'Not yet. You'll just have to wait.'

Willow and the others gave up asking him. They were all keen to see what was in their parcels.

'Look!' whinnied Sapphire, opening hers with her horn. 'Mum's sent me some ribbons for my mane to bring me luck!' She held up ten pale pink ribbons in her mouth.

'And I've got a cake to cheer me up while I'm working so hard!' said Storm, holding up a large iced cake by the red ribbon that was wrapped around it. 'We can all share it.'

Willow pulled out her present. It was a necklace made of delicate white shells. 'Oh, wow! I've got a necklace!' She read the letter inside the parcel:

Dear Willow,
Your dad and I know how hard you have been working for your exams and we are sending you this little present so that you know we're thinking about

you. Just do your best and try hard and we'll be very proud of you. Good luck! Love from Mum and Dad XXX

A warm glow spread through Willow. It was lovely to know her mum and dad were thinking about her. She glanced at Troy. He didn't look very happy.

'What does your letter say?' Willow nudged him gently with her horn. 'Is it what you were expecting?'

'No,' sighed Troy. 'It doesn't say anything about what I asked. It's from my dad not my mum and it's just about the exams. Look.' He pushed the letter towards Willow. She read it.

Dear Troy,
Your mother and I hope you are revising hard for your examinations. We hardly need to remind you how important it is that you do well in all your subjects. As Prince of Arcadia you must set an example to others. We

wish you all the best of luck and look forward to hearing of your great achievements.

Your loving father, King of Arcadia

Willow thought about her own letter and couldn't help feeling a bit sorry for Troy. She knew that as long as she tried her best in the exams her parents would be proud of her, no matter how she did, but Troy's father made it sound like he would only be happy if Troy did really well.

'What am I going to do?' Troy said. He took the letter and looked at it again. 'What if I do badly in my exams, Willow?'

'You won't,' Willow said encouragingly. 'You're really good at everything, particularly flying.'

'I suppose I am OK at most things. It's just history I find really hard,' Troy said. 'What if I fail?'

All the Year One unicorns took flying, charms and transformation classes and then they could choose three other subjects from weather magic, healing, rose-quartz gazing and history. Willow and Troy were the only ones of the friends who did history.

'Oh, Troy. You won't fail,' said Sapphire, listening in.

Troy stamped a hoof. 'What do you know about it, Sapphire? You don't even do history. You've no idea how hard it is!'

Sapphire looked hurt.

'Troy! Don't get cross with Sapphire!' Storm protested. 'It's not her fault you find history hard. Anyway, you chose to do it. You could have done a different subject.'

'No, I couldn't!' Troy exclaimed. 'My parents wouldn't let me. They think that because I'm Prince it's really important that I know about the past and what has happened in Arcadia. I had to do history but I'm no good at it!'

'Don't worry. I'll help you,' Willow said quickly. 'We can revise together this week.'

Troy gave her a grateful look. 'Thanks, Willow.' He touched noses with Sapphire. 'And I'm sorry I got cross with you, Sapphire. I'm just a bit nervous.'

'That's all right,' Sapphire whickered gently.

Troy sighed. 'The sooner these exams are over the better.'

Willow couldn't agree more!

Chapter Two

Helping Troy

'**R**ight, everyone. Next question.'
Roswell, the pretty young
teacher who taught history, looked
around at the class of Year Ones
who were gathered in the classroom.
'Who won the War of the Great
River? Was it the ogres or the trolls?'
Willow put up her horn.

'Yes, Willow.'

'The ogres,' Willow replied.

'Very good.' Roswell nodded approvingly. 'That's the fifth question you've answered correctly today. You've obviously been revising hard. Well done.' Willow glowed with pride.

Roswell walked to the front of the room. 'Now let's have a look at what happened.' She touched her horn to a large slab of shining white quartz. The surface of it seemed to shimmer and a moving picture appeared. It showed two armies, one made up of trolls and one of ogres. They were attacking each other with huge wooden clubs. As the

class watched, the ogres began to
chase the trolls away. Then one of
the trolls turned as if it was looking
straight at them and roared, showing
jagged yellow teeth. Willow shivered.
She preferred it when Roswell
showed them bits of history with
animals and pixies and birds.

Roswell touched her horn to the
quartz and it went blank again.
'Now, next question,' she continued.

'Which royal unicorn negotiated a truce between the pixies and the water sprites at the Rushing River twenty years ago?'

Several unicorns, including Willow, put up their horns but Roswell was looking at Troy. 'Troy!'

Willow felt Troy jump beside her. He'd been staring out of the window. She was sure from the guilty look on his face that he'd been thinking about flying.

'You haven't answered any questions yet, Troy,' Roswell said to him. 'Can you tell me the answer to this one?'

'Um . . . it was . . . it was . . .' Troy stammered.

'Randulf the Twelfth,' Willow hissed under her breath.

'Rudolph the Third!' Troy said, mis-hearing her.

'No!' Roswell said crossly. 'Rudolph the Third died a hundred years ago!' Some of the other unicorns giggled. 'Really, Troy. You should have been able to answer that question. It was Randulf the Twelfth – your own uncle!'

'Uncle Ulf?' Troy looked astonished. 'He negotiated a truce? That's amazing! It takes him an hour every dinnertime to decide between apples and carrots!'

The rest of the class giggled even louder. But Roswell didn't look amused. 'This is not good enough, Troy. If you can't answer a simple question like the one I've just asked, however do you think you will pass the exam?'

Troy hung his head. Roswell walked to the front and again touched her horn to the white quartz. This time the rock shimmered into a picture of a sparkling silver river rushing over a waterfall. A handsome, sporty-looking unicorn, who looked quite like Troy, stood beside it and all along the riverbank tiny pixies and water sprites were dancing and swinging each other round by the hands.

Roswell continued asking questions and showing scenes from Arcadia's history. Troy didn't say anything else for the rest of the lesson. Willow noticed that he was looking very down. 'Are you OK?' she asked him in concern when the lesson finished.

He shook his head. 'What am I going to do, Willow? I'm never going to pass the exam. I'm rubbish at history!'

'You're not rubbish. You just need to go through your notes and start learning them,' said Willow.

'But I haven't got any notes!' Troy said despairingly. 'Look!' He gave his history book to Willow. She put it on the floor and turned the pages.

There were some notes at the beginning but the later pages were filled with pictures of flying unicorns.

'Troy!' she said. 'You haven't been listening at all in lessons, have you?'

'Not really,' he said in a small voice.

Willow felt cross with him but she

could see that wasn't going to help. 'All right, look, you can borrow my notes. Meet me in the library at lunchtime and you can start copying them out. I'll explain anything you don't understand.'

'Thanks,' sighed Troy.

As soon as it was lunchtime, Willow went to the library. She was very hungry and really wanted her lunch, but helping Troy was more important. She decided she would grab some mouthfuls of grass in the meadows before afternoon lessons started. Getting her history books out, she waited impatiently for Troy to arrive.

Fifteen minutes went by, twenty

minutes, twenty-five minutes . . .
Willow got increasingly worried.
Where was Troy? Why hadn't he
turned up? Then suddenly Troy
came trotting into the library. 'Sorry
I'm late!' he gasped.

'Where have you been?' demanded
Willow. 'I've been really worried
about you. I've been waiting ages.'

Troy looked a bit sheepish. 'Umm
. . . I've . . . well, I've been at flying
practice.'

Willow stared. 'Flying practice!'

Troy nodded. 'The Tricorn's asked
the Flying Team to do a display at
the end of term when the parents
arrive, so we've got to practise every
day.'

Willow couldn't believe it. She'd
missed lunch and had been waiting
around in the library all because
Troy had been flying! 'I thought you
wanted to pass your history exam!'
She began throwing books into her
bag. 'I've been here all lunchtime.
You could have told me you were
going flying and then I'd have gone
and done something else. Well, you

can forget about me helping you from now on!'

'Willow, wait!' Troy said quickly. 'I just didn't think. Please help me. I'm sorry you missed lunch. Look, stay here – just for one minute!' And, before Willow could protest, he had cantered out of the door. She frowned. Where was he going?

A few minutes later Troy came back with a bag of apples and carrots in his mouth. 'I got these from the elves in the kitchens. I *am* really sorry I didn't come earlier. Please will you still help me, Willow?'

He did look very sorry and Willow felt her anger fade. 'OK,' she said, biting into an apple. 'Thank you for the food. Shall we do some history then?'

Troy nodded. 'Yes, please.'

Their revision session wasn't a success, however. Willow tried to explain her notes but, every time she started talking, Troy stared into the distance and his eyes grew vacant.

'Are you listening to me, Troy?' Willow demanded when he had failed to answer a question for the third time.

'Mmm . . . what?' Troy blinked. 'Oh, sorry. It's just so hard. If only we knew what the exam questions were going to be – then we could just learn the answers to those questions.'

'You know it doesn't work like that,' Willow told him. 'We have to learn everything.'

'But there's just so much of it,' said Troy. 'I'm never going to be able to remember it all!'

'You will,' said Willow confidently. 'You just have to keep trying.'

A horn blew outside, signalling the end of lunchtime. Willow shut her books and sighed. 'Come on. We can do some more later.'

She left the library with Troy walking slowly behind her.

Sapphire's Idea

When Willow and Troy arrived at the Charm Fields for their afternoon lesson, Sapphire and Storm were already waiting for them. 'How did your revising go?' asked Storm as they met up.

'Not great,' Troy sighed. 'There's just so much to learn. I wish I knew what the exam questions were going to be but I guess there's no chance of that. I could never get to see them – not when the elves have all the exam papers in big chests in the mail room.'

'And even if you *could* see them, that would be cheating,' Willow reminded him.

'Not really. I wouldn't be looking at the answers, just the questions,' said Troy.

'It would still be cheating,' said Willow. 'Anyway, it's silly even thinking about it. There's no way of seeing the exam papers before the exam.'

'I suppose you could always . . .' Sapphire broke off.

Troy looked at her curiously. 'You could what?'

'It doesn't matter,' said Sapphire, shaking her head.

Willow glanced at her, wondering what she'd been about to say. But just then Damaris, the charms teacher, flew down. 'OK, gather round, everyone!' she whinnied. 'We've got a lot of work to get through today!'

Willow moved forward with the

other Year Ones. It seemed like there was a lot to do every day at the moment!

For the whole of the charms lesson they practised making Good Luck and Good Health charms and then they had a transformation class. Transformation meant turning one thing into another. That day they were revising how to turn acorns into different types of food and flowers. Tor, the teacher, made them do it over and over again until they got it right.

By the end of the class Willow's head was spinning. She'd been planning on revising before supper but decided to go for a walk instead. She looked round for the others to see if they wanted to go with her but Storm had already gone off with Flint to practise some weather magic, and Sapphire and Troy were nowhere to be seen, so Willow set off on her own.

Carefully, she picked her way down to the beach. She loved walking along the sparkling white sands and watching the crystal-clear waves lapping against the shore. When she reached the beach, she breathed in deeply. The Rose Quartz

Cliffs that towered above the white sands glimmered pink in the afternoon sunlight. It was very peaceful. *School's such hard work at the moment*, Willow thought as she began to walk along the beach. *I wish the exams were over.*

After the exams there was just one week left of term, with all sorts of fun activities planned – a picnic in the woods, a moonlight swim in the sea, a magic tournament in the Assembly Fields. The unicorns would then all get their exam results and break up for the summer holidays the next day. Willow snorted. It was weird to imagine spending six weeks without

Sapphire, Storm and Troy. She'd got so used to seeing them every day. *I'll really miss them*, Willow realized. *I wish we could see each other in the holidays* . . .

She broke off from her thoughts as she noticed two unicorns standing near the cliffs a bit further along the beach. They were deep in conversation, their backs to the sea, so it took a while before Willow realized it was Troy and Sapphire! What were they doing? She was about to whinny but stopped herself. It would be much more fun to creep up on them instead and make them jump! She trotted over as quietly as she could.

Maybe they're about to do some rose-quartz gazing, Willow thought.

Unicorns could see anyone anywhere in Arcadia if they touched their horns to a rock of rose quartz and said the name of that person. Sapphire, who took rose-quartz gazing as one of her subjects, was very good at it.

As Willow got closer, she slowed to a walk and picked her way quietly over the rocks towards them.

'I *think* I could do it,' Sapphire was saying to Troy. 'I've been wondering about it all afternoon. It will be difficult because it's not like seeing a person, but I bet it's possible.'

'Are you sure you don't mind?' said Troy slowly.

'I'm sure,' said Sapphire. 'I know how worried you are and that it would really help you.'

Willow frowned. What were they talking about?

'OK, here goes,' said Sapphire, stepping up to the cliff. She touched her horn to the rose quartz and whispered something under her breath that Willow couldn't quite hear. For a long moment Sapphire concentrated hard and then the rock shimmered and she gave a little gasp. 'Look. It's working, Troy! A picture's coming.'

Troy caught his breath. 'I can see the papers in the chest! I can read them, Sapphire! Oh, wow!'

Willow crept closer. Her eyes widened as she saw the picture in the rose quartz – it was an exam paper lying inside a big wooden chest. An exam paper with the heading: *Year One: History Exam*.

'What are you two doing?' she whinnied.

Sapphire and Troy both jumped about a metre in the air. They swung round, their faces full of guilt.

'Willow!' Troy exclaimed. 'What are you doing here?'

Willow ignored the question. 'You're cheating!' she cried. 'You're using rose quartz to look at the exam papers!'

'Only the history one,' said Troy defensively. 'And I was just having a quick look. I wanted to see the questions so I know what to revise. I wasn't looking at the answer papers.'

'It's still cheating! You know it is!' Willow stared at him furiously and then swung round to Sapphire.

'Sapphire! How could you use your magic for something like that?'

Sapphire looked very flustered. 'I . . . I just thought it would help Troy. I knew how worried he was and I thought if I used my rose-quartz gazing skills to help him, it would be a nice thing to do. I . . . I didn't think it was that bad.'

'Well, it is!' said Willow.

'Don't be angry with Sapphire,' Troy said quickly.

'I'm not!' Willow exclaimed. And she wasn't really. She knew that, although it was wrong of Sapphire, she'd only done it because she was kind and didn't like seeing Troy unhappy. 'I'm angry with *you*! I can't believe you'd let Sapphire use her magic so you could cheat.'

'It was only a little look.' Troy tossed his head. 'You're making a huge fuss about nothing. You're such a goody-goody!'

'I am not!' Willow spluttered indignantly.

'I suppose you're going to tell the teachers now,' Troy said, his expression half-daring, half-scared.

'No,' said Willow, thinking that she wanted to, but knowing that she couldn't get her friends into trouble like that.

Troy looked very relieved. 'Thanks. Well, I'm going to go to the library

to write down the questions before
I forget them.'

'But . . .' Willow began.

It was too late. Troy had already
flown into the air and was galloping
away.

Chapter
Four

Keeping Secrets

Willow stared speechlessly after
Troy. Beside her, Sapphire
gave a distressed whinny. 'I shouldn't
have used the rose quartz to look. I
feel awful now. I was only trying to
help.'

'I know,' Willow said. She took a
deep breath and felt her anger fade.

'It's not your fault, Sapphire. Not really. Troy shouldn't have let you use your magic to cheat.'

'Don't tell anyone,' begged Sapphire. 'I know you said you wouldn't tell the teachers, but please don't say anything to anyone – not even Storm.'

'We can't *not* tell Storm!' Willow protested. 'He's our best friend.'

'But I really don't want him to know,' said Sapphire. 'I feel so bad and it makes Troy look bad too.' Willow hesitated.

'Please, Willow,' Sapphire begged.

'OK,' Willow sighed, although she didn't like it. 'I won't tell Storm.'

★

When Willow and Sapphire got
back from the beach, they went
to have their supper. All meals
at Unicorn School were served
on four long tables in the
Moonlight Meadows. There were
holes for buckets in the tabletops
and the unicorns were allowed to
eat as much as they wanted. That
evening the buckets were filled
with a warm bran mash, carrots

and apples. Willow and Sapphire
found two places just as Troy
arrived. He came to stand beside
them.

'Hi,' he said.

'Hi,' muttered Sapphire awkwardly,
but Willow turned her back on him.

'Aren't you talking to me?' Troy
said.

'No,' replied Willow.

Storm came trotting over. 'Hi, guys!'

he whinnied as he joined them at the table. 'What have you been doing?'

Sapphire, Willow and Troy all spoke at the same time.

'N–nothing,' Sapphire gabbled.

'We've been at the beach,' muttered Willow.

'I've been revising,' said Troy.

Storm looked surprised. 'Oh, right. So you've all been doing different things then?'

'Yes,' said Sapphire.

'No,' said Troy.

'Sort of,' said Willow.

Storm looked confused.

'What have you been doing, Storm?' Willow asked, to change the subject.

'I've been practising flying,' Storm

laughed. 'I'm so useless at it I'm sure I'm going to fail the exam, so I went to talk to Atlas about it after lessons. He was really nice and gave me some exercises to practise. He also said he'll give me some extra teaching between now and the exams. I'm going to get up early and have a lesson every morning before school starts.'

'That's really good,' Sapphire said encouragingly.

Willow nodded. 'Yes, it'll be hard work but I bet you'll end up passing the exam.' She shot a meaningful look at Troy. 'It's much better than *cheating*.' Troy looked uncomfortable.

'Of course it is!' said Storm.

'Cheating's dreadful! I'd never do that.'

'No, me neither,' said Willow, still looking at Troy.

Troy cleared his throat. 'I'm not feeling very hungry,' he said. 'I . . . I think I might give supper a miss tonight.' And, with that, he left the table and hurried away.

Storm looked surprised. 'It's not like Troy to miss supper. Do you think he's all right? Maybe I should go after him.'

'No, don't,' Willow said, knowing that it was the talk of cheating that had made Troy leave the table. 'He'll be fine.'

'But he said he didn't feel hungry,' Storm said.

'He'll be fine,' repeated Willow.

Storm frowned at her. 'What's going on? You're behaving really strangely.'

'It's nothing,' Willow muttered.

'Nothing at all,' Sapphire added quickly. 'Mmm.' She dug her nose into her feed bucket. 'This bran mash is delicious!'

'Yes, these apples are really yummy,' said Willow.

Storm looked from one to the other. 'There's something you're not telling me, isn't there?' When neither of them said anything, he looked upset. Burying his nose in his bucket, he didn't say another word for the rest of the meal.

Over the next week Willow only really talked to Sapphire. She was still very cross with Troy and wouldn't speak to him, and Storm was clearly upset with all three of them. Willow felt awful about not telling him what had happened but she couldn't go back on her promise to Sapphire. She ended up spending most of her time in the library. It was good to get lots of revision done but she did miss hanging out with Troy and Storm. It was always more fun when the four of them were doing things together.

At long last the exams started. They were being held in the Great Hall, where desks were lined up in rows. On each of them was a question paper, turned over so the unicorns couldn't see the questions until the exam started. There was also a sheet of sparkling white parchment to write the answers on and a silver inkwell full of purple ink. The unicorns would write by dipping their horns into the ink. For most of their subjects, apart from history, the Year Ones had two exams – one where they had to go to the hall and write the answers down, and one where they had to go outside and actually do magic to show what they had learnt.

Although Willow was very nervous when the exams first started, she soon found that they weren't really that scary. She didn't know every answer on every exam paper but she had a feeling she was doing well and, by the end of the week, she was almost beginning to enjoy herself. Even better, her friends seemed to be doing OK too. Sapphire came out of the rose-quartz gazing exam looking very happy and Storm had been practising his flying so much that he managed to do almost everything Atlas asked.

The very last exam was history. Willow and Troy stood next to each other without speaking as they waited outside the Great Hall to be let in.

Roswell opened the big wooden doors. 'You may all come through now,' she said.

Troy glanced at Willow. 'Good luck.'

Willow hesitated. She couldn't bring herself to wish him luck too. *It's not as if he needs it anyway*, she told herself. *After all, he knows what the questions are going to be.* Avoiding his eyes, she hurried past him into the hall and found her desk. The exam was about to begin!

Chapter Five

Who's Been Cheating?

When all the unicorns were at their desks, Roswell tossed her head in the air and a stream of silver stars flew out of her horn. When Willow had first seen a teacher do this at the start of an exam, she had been amazed, but now she was used to it. Each silver star landed on an exam paper. They twinkled for a moment and then vanished with a faint *pop*. The papers magically flipped over so the unicorns could read the questions and the exam began!

'*Question 1: In what year did the Battle of the High Peaks start and what role did the dragons have to play in it?*'

Easy, thought Willow, dipping her horn into the inkwell. She heard a faint gasp from beside her and looked at Troy. He was staring at the exam paper, his eyes wide.

Willow wondered what the matter was. But there was no time to think about it now. She knew they only

had an hour to answer all the
questions and she had to start
writing.

For the rest of the hour Willow
hardly looked up from her exam
paper, but she was aware that,

beside her, Troy was sighing and shifting restlessly from side to side. He seemed to finish writing very early.

When the exam ended and Roswell collected in all the papers, Troy cantered out of the hall, pushing past the other unicorns in his hurry to get out. Willow frowned. He didn't look very happy.

She made her way over to the Moonlight Meadows. Sapphire was waiting at the lunch table. Her exams had finished the day before. 'How did it go?' she asked Willow eagerly. 'I've been thinking about you and Troy all morning.'

'It wasn't too bad. I could answer most of the questions,' Willow said.

'I guess Troy could answer them all,' said Sapphire.

'Well, it was a bit odd.' Willow told Sapphire about Troy's shocked look when he saw the question paper and the way he had cantered off afterwards.

'That's weird.' Sapphire frowned. 'I wonder why he did that?'

'I don't know. You'd think that he'd have been looking really happy. After all, he knew all the —' Just then Storm arrived and Willow quickly shut up.

Storm glanced at them curiously. 'What are you two talking about?'

'Nothing,' Willow muttered.

'Nothing you want *me* to hear anyway,' Storm huffed, looking hurt. 'I was going to ask you how your exam went but I guess there's no point. You probably won't tell me that either!'

Willow felt awful. 'Of course I'll tell you about the exam,' she began, but she broke off as an elf walked into the meadow and blew on a horn.

'What's going on?' Sapphire said in surprise.

Willow didn't know. This didn't usually happen. Her eyes widened as the Tricorn, a snow-white unicorn and the school's head teacher, came into the Moonlight Meadows. The Tricorn's horn was striped gold, silver and bronze and today there was an unusually serious expression on his noble face.

He stopped and looked around gravely. 'Good afternoon, everyone.

I am sorry to delay the start of your lunch but I have some very disturbing news. It appears that last week someone used rose quartz to look into the chest containing the Year One history exam papers.'

There was a gasp from the unicorns. Willow's stomach felt as if it had just been flooded with icy water. She glanced quickly at Sapphire.

'There is a spell placed on all the exam chests,' the Tricorn continued. 'It tells the elves when magic has been used by someone trying to cheat. When the elves opened the history chest this morning, they discovered that someone had been dishonest enough to try and use magic to look inside.'

A chorus of whispers ran round the listening unicorns.

'Who was it?'

'Who could it be?'

'Who would have done something like that?'

Willow kept her eyes to the ground. She didn't dare look up. She was sure that if anyone saw her face they would realize that she knew the answer.

'This is obviously extremely serious,' the Tricorn said gravely. 'The other teachers and I can use magic to discover exactly who used rose quartz to try and cheat, but

first I want to give that unicorn
the chance to come forward. If no
one has confessed by tomorrow
evening then we will begin work
on the reveal spell and discover
who it was.'

Willow glanced up just as the Tricorn looked around at them all, his eyes concentrating particularly on the Year Ones. 'I will *not* have cheating in this school,' he said firmly. 'We will find out who did this. If it is you, I urge you to come forward before it is too late.'

Turning round, the Tricorn walked quickly out of the meadows.

Chapter Six

What Should Sapphire Do?

As soon as the Tricorn had gone, the unicorns at all four tables started talking in whispers about who could have cheated.

'I can't believe it,' said Storm to Willow and Sapphire, forgetting about their earlier quarrel. 'It's got to be someone in your history class,

Willow. Who could it be?' Willow shrugged. Sapphire was looking as if she felt sick.

'I suppose it's got to be someone who also does rose-quartz gazing,' continued Storm thoughtfully. 'Who does both? Topaz, Starlight and Moondust all do both subjects, don't they?'

'I . . . it needn't be one of them,' Sapphire stammered quickly. 'Any unicorn can use rose quartz.'

'Yes, but I bet you'd have to be really good at it to be able to look in the chest,' said Storm. 'Hmm, now who could it be?'

Willow wasn't listening. She had caught sight of a figure in the

shadows of the nearby apple trees.
'Troy!' she exclaimed.

'No, it couldn't be Troy,' said Storm,
thinking she was talking to him. 'He's
no good at rose-quartz gazing. And
anyway, he wouldn't cheat.'

'I'll be back in a minute,' Willow
said, setting off towards the trees.

She broke into a canter. Troy saw
her coming and turned to go. 'Troy!

Wait!' Willow whinnied. But he
didn't. He flew into the sky.

Willow chased after him as he shot
away towards the clouds. There was
no way she could keep up with him
– he was much better at flying than
she was – but she was determined
not to let him get away completely.
She gritted her teeth and galloped
after him as he twisted and turned
through the air and tried to lose her.

'Troy! Come back!' she shouted crossly. 'I want to talk to you!'

Willow knew that he couldn't go on flying forever and at last he landed on the beach. Willow flew down beside him. She was panting hard.

'What do you want?' Troy said defensively.

'Did you hear what the Tricorn said?'

'Yes.' Troy looked uncomfortable.

'They know that someone has looked inside the chest. If they use magic to find out who it was, they'll see Sapphire!'

'It's not a big deal, Willow,' Troy said quickly. 'It's not like Sapphire does history. She can just say that she was rose-quartz gazing and . . . and looked into the chest by accident!'

Willow stared at him. 'Oh, yes, they're *really* going to believe that!'

'They might,' Troy said hopefully.

'They won't, Troy! They'll think she was trying to cheat for one of her other subjects but the magic went wrong. You *have* to own up,' Willow said. 'You can't go ahead and get full marks for your history exam while Sapphire gets into trouble!'

'I'm sure she won't get into trouble and I know I'm not going to get full marks,' Troy said. 'I've failed the paper.'

Willow was so surprised that for a moment her anger left her. 'What do you mean? How can you have failed?'

'I don't know. Maybe Sapphire's rose-quartz gazing magic wasn't good enough,' said Troy. 'But the questions we had to answer weren't the same ones I saw when I looked at the exam paper in the chest. None of the questions I'd learnt came up.' He groaned. 'I can't own up, Willow. It's going to be bad enough that I've failed the exam without being caught for cheating too. What would my father say if he was told that?'

Willow knew it was hard for him but he *couldn't* let Sapphire take the blame. Despite what Troy said, she was sure everyone would think Sapphire had been trying to cheat. 'You have to tell the Tricorn it was you,' she told him.

Troy looked scared. 'I can't.' He shook his head. 'No, I . . . I won't!'

Willow stamped a hoof furiously. 'Then I don't want to be your friend any more.' She turned round and flew away.

'Willow!' Troy called after her.

But Willow didn't stop or turn round. *Maybe I should tell the Tricorn the truth*, she wondered. But the thought made her feel cold inside. She hated the idea of telling tales . . .

Feeling too worried to eat, she didn't go back to the lunch table but headed to the cloud stables. Sapphire was there with Storm. He was looking very concerned. 'If you're feeling ill, Sapphire, you should tell one of the teachers,' he was saying as Willow walked into the stable. 'Please let me go and get one of them.'

Sapphire shook her head. 'No, please don't.'

Storm saw Willow. 'Willow, where did you go? Sapphire says she's feeling really ill but she won't let me tell a teacher.'

Willow and Sapphire looked at each other.

'Tell her that she should let us get someone,' Storm said.

'No,' Sapphire said quickly.

'Let's not,' said Willow.

'But why?' demanded Storm.

When neither of them said anything, he looked cross. 'Oh, this is another of your little secrets, is it?' He stormed out of the stable, pushing past Willow and cantering down the corridor.

'Oh, Willow!' Sapphire burst out.

'This is dreadful. I don't know what to do. The Tricorn's going to find out that I was the one who looked in the chest.'

'You're going to have to go and tell him the truth — tell him that you did it for Troy,' said Willow.

Sapphire looked horrified. 'I can't do that! Troy will get into real trouble.'

'But if you don't, they might think you were trying to cheat for yourself and that the magic just went wrong,' said Willow. 'It *is* Troy's fault.'

Sapphire looked wretched. 'I can't do it. I can't!' Tears welled in her eyes.

Willow nuzzled her. If only
Sapphire had never suggested
looking in the rose quartz. If only
Troy had said no when she *had*
suggested it! Now everything had
gone wrong. She wasn't friends with
Troy any more and Storm was angry
with her and Sapphire was going to
get into loads of trouble . . .

'I wish none of this had ever happened,' Sapphire said unhappily.

'So do I,' sighed Willow.

'I do too.'

They turned round. Storm had come back without them realizing. 'Why won't you tell me what's going on?' he asked them. 'I thought we weren't supposed to keep secrets from each other.'

'We're not supposed to.' Willow looked at Sapphire. 'Please tell him.'

Sapphire hesitated and then nodded. 'I'm sorry, Storm. Willow's been wanting to tell you what's been going on but I said we couldn't because I felt really awful and it makes Troy look bad.'

'Why?' said Storm.

'Listen and I'll tell you everything,' Sapphire said. And she did.

Storm listened in astonishment. 'I can't believe Troy cheated like that! But surely he's going to own up now he knows the Tricorn's found out about it.'

Willow shook her head. 'He won't.'

Storm looked at Sapphire. 'Then you have to tell the Tricorn what happened,' he said firmly. 'They're sure to think you were trying to cheat. You can't take the blame and it's not fair of Troy to expect you to. If you won't tell the Tricorn then I will. I'll go and find him right now.'

Sapphire hesitated and looked at Willow.

'Storm's right,' Willow said. 'You should tell the Tricorn the truth.'

Sapphire took a deep breath. 'OK. I don't want to but I will.'

'It's the right thing to do,' Storm said, nuzzling her. 'Do you want us to come with you?'

Sapphire shook her head.

'Good luck,' Willow told her.

Sapphire gulped. 'Thanks. I think I'm going to need it!'

Chapter Seven

Telling the Truth

Willow and Storm waited anxiously for Sapphire to come back. After a little while they heard the door opening.

'How did it . . . ?' Willow broke off. It wasn't Sapphire. It was Troy. 'Oh,' she said shortly. 'It's you.' Troy headed for his stall.

'Willow and Sapphire have told me what happened,' Storm said, stepping out in front of him.

Troy stopped. 'They told you!'

Storm nodded. 'I can't believe it, Troy. You tried to cheat and now you won't own up to it. That's awful.'

'It's all right for you, Storm. Your father isn't the King of Arcadia . . .' Troy protested.

'That doesn't make any difference!' Storm exclaimed. 'You shouldn't have done it. I don't think I want to be friends with you any more. How can you let Sapphire take the blame?'

'I told you — I don't think she'll have to,' Troy said desperately. 'The Tricorn knows she doesn't do history.'

'But he'll think she was trying to cheat anyway,' Storm said.

'You should have confessed,' said Willow. 'It's too late now anyway. Sapphire's gone to tell the Tricorn what really happened.'

Troy stared at her in horror. 'She hasn't!'

'She has,' said Storm. 'She didn't want to, but I told her that if she didn't, I would.'

The door opened. This time it *was* Sapphire. She was looking very upset and big tears were rolling down her nose.

'Sapphire! What happened?' Willow asked. 'What did the Tricorn say?'

'He said that he couldn't tolerate cheating and that I might be sent home from school and not be allowed to come back.' A loud sob escaped Sapphire.

'What?' Storm burst out. 'But surely he must have realized you weren't cheating – you don't even do history.'

'I . . . I didn't tell the truth,' Sapphire said. 'I couldn't.' She glanced at Troy. 'When I told the Tricorn it had been me who looked into the chest, he asked why I had looked at the history exam. I just couldn't get Troy into so much trouble so I just said my magic went wrong. I'd been trying to look at the charms exams and had made a mistake.'

'So the Tricorn thinks you really *were* trying to cheat,' Willow said in dismay.

'Yes,' Sapphire whispered.

Willow swung round to Troy.

'Troy! You can't let Sapphire take the blame! You . . .'

But Troy was already walking towards Sapphire. 'Don't worry, Sapphire,' he said, interrupting Willow. 'You've been a really good friend. It was very brave of you not to tell the Tricorn the truth to try and stop me getting into trouble, but I can't let you be punished. I honestly didn't think you would be, but if the Tricorn really does think you were cheating then I'll go and see him straight away.'

'But, Troy! You'll be sent home!' protested Sapphire.

'I deserve to be.' Troy's voice shook. 'This is all my fault.'

Willow breathed out. 'Oh, Troy.'

He swallowed. 'I've been really stupid. I'm not surprised you don't want to be my friends. I wouldn't want to be my friend either.'

Willow hurried forward and touched him with her nose. 'You know, I actually *do* want to be friends with you now.'

'Me too!' Storm joined them. 'You're being really brave.'

Sapphire nodded.

Troy looked round at them all. 'Will you still be friends with me, even if I'm sent home?' They all nodded.

'And we'll come with you to see the Tricorn,' said Sapphire. 'Whatever he says, we'll be with you.'

Troy managed a small smile.
'Thank you,' he said.

The Tricorn's study was just beside
the Great Hall. Troy knocked on the
door with his horn.

'Come in,' the Tricorn called.

Troy pushed the door open and all
four unicorns trotted in.

The Tricorn was standing behind
his big wooden desk. 'Hello,' he said.
'What can I do for you?'

'I've got something to tell you,
Tricorn.' Troy swallowed nervously. 'I
. . . it . . . well, Sapphire wasn't
cheating.' The words suddenly
rushed out of him. 'She did use her
magic to look inside the history

chest but it was to help me. I was
the one who was cheating. Punish
me, but please, please don't send
Sapphire home. She didn't look to
try and cheat herself!'

'I know.' The Tricorn's deep voice
was very serious.

'You know!' Troy stared.

'Someone who is as good at rose-quartz gazing as Sapphire would never make such a mistake as looking into the wrong chest,' said the Tricorn. 'I knew she wasn't telling me the truth.' He looked at Sapphire. 'I hope you have learnt a lesson from this, Sapphire. You must never again use your magic to help someone cheat.'

Sapphire bit her lip. 'I'm sorry. I promise I'll *never* do it again.'

'Then we will say no more about it,' said the Tricorn in a more kindly voice. He looked at Troy. 'And now for you.'

'I know you're going to send me

home.' Troy hung his head. 'But I deserve it.'

'I'm not going to send you home, Troy,' the Tricorn said.

Troy looked up in surprise. 'What?'

'You have behaved very badly but at the end of the day, when it looked like your friend was going to be in trouble, you came forward and told the truth. Because of that I am going to give you a second chance. You may stay here at Unicorn School, although you will have to retake your history exam in a week's time.'

'That's the day before we break up!' said Troy.

'Yes,' the Tricorn replied. 'I am

afraid if you are going to do the work needed to pass you will have to miss out on many of the end-of-term activities.'

'That's OK!' Troy gasped. 'I don't care. I'll work and work and work. I just want to pass the exam and do it without cheating.'

'I'll help you,' Willow promised. 'We can use my notes – properly this time!'

'We'll help too,' Storm said, looking at Sapphire, who nodded.

'We might not do history ourselves but we can help by testing you,' she said.

'Thank you!' Troy told them gratefully. He looked at the Tricorn.

'And thank you for giving me another chance.'

'I believe that courage should be rewarded and it must have taken a great deal of that for you to come and own up,' the Tricorn said. 'If you pass the exam, nothing more will be said about this whole incident, and I will not mention it to your parents.' Troy looked very relieved.

'You may go now,' the Tricorn told him. 'Work hard, Troy.'

'I will,' Troy promised seriously. 'And I'll never cheat ever again.' He turned to go and then stopped, frowning. 'Please may I just ask you one thing?'

The Tricorn nodded. 'Of course.'

'Well, the history exam paper I saw – when Sapphire used the rose quartz – it . . . it was different from the one in the exam. Why was that?'

The Tricorn gave a small laugh. 'That was because all of the chests have a deception charm on them as well as a cheating spell. Not only do the elves know when someone has been looking at the paper dishonestly, but the paper itself shows the wrong questions – so the unicorn who is cheating does not prosper.' He leant forward, suddenly serious. 'You surely do not think you are the first unicorn to have thought of using rose quartz to cheat, Troy? Magic can be very tempting at times. Just remember to use it only for good in the future.' His expression softened. 'Now go.'

As soon as the door was shut behind them, Troy breathed a huge sigh of relief. 'Phew! I don't have to go home! Will you all help me revise for the exam like you said?'

'Of course!' Willow, Sapphire and Storm chorused.

Troy looked determined. 'I'm going to work so hard. I'm going to pass this exam. I have to!'

Chapter Eight

The End of Term!

'OK, Troy. Who were the two leaders in the Battle of the Dragons?' Willow looked at Troy.

'Fangtooth and Gracken,' Troy replied promptly.

'Which unicorn first discovered the magic of rose-quartz gazing?' Sapphire asked.

'Queen Starbright the Second,' answered Troy.

'And who is believed to be the fastest unicorn ever?' questioned Storm.

Troy tossed his mane. 'That's easy – Silverhoof. He won every race there ever was while he was at school and he holds the record for being the fastest unicorn to fly around Misty Mountain and the fastest unicorn to fly from the High Winds Pass to the palace.'

Willow felt a rush of relief. It was five days since Troy had confessed to the Tricorn that he had cheated and since then he had been working really hard. First he had copied out all his missing history notes and then he had tried to learn everything so he could remember it in the exam. Willow, Storm and Sapphire had spent every minute they could testing him and it finally looked as if all the hard work was beginning to pay off. Every question

they had asked that day Troy had
got right!

'You're doing so well,' Willow told
him.

'Thanks to all of you,' Troy said
gratefully. 'I'd never have been able
to learn so much without your help.
You've been brilliant friends. You've
missed all the fun end-of-term stuff
to help me.'

'You've missed out on everything
too,' Storm told him. 'You even
pulled out of the Flying Team
display and I know you really
wanted to do that.'

'I couldn't have gone to all the
practices *and* revised like I needed
to,' Troy said.

'I can't believe the exam is tomorrow,' said Storm.

Troy looked anxious. 'Neither can I.'

'You'll be OK,' Sapphire reassured him.

Troy gulped. 'I hope you're right,' he said.

The next morning Troy went nervously into the hall to sit his exam. All the other exams had finished and he was the only unicorn in there. As Roswell shut the door, Willow thought how lonely Troy looked, standing behind a desk in the huge room, all on his own.

'I hope he gets the questions

right,' she said anxiously to Sapphire and Storm.

Storm nodded. 'I'm more nervous about Troy doing this exam than I am about getting my own exam results this afternoon.' Willow knew just how Storm felt!

The hour of the exam seemed to take forever to go by. Storm paced up and down, Willow fidgeted anxiously and Sapphire kept sighing in a worried way. At long last it was over. The door opened and Troy came trotting out. His ears were pricked and his eyes were bright.

'Well?' Willow demanded.

'It was actually OK!' Troy burst out. 'There were a few questions that I couldn't do but all the others were fine!'

'Phew!' Sapphire said, tossing her mane with relief.

'That's brilliant!' said Storm.

'I'm just glad it's over,' said Troy. 'Come on, let's get out of here and go outside!' They cantered happily out to the meadows. The sun was shining and the other unicorns in the school were all out enjoying themselves.

'Have you heard the news?' Oriel, a Year Three unicorn, came racing over to them. 'The Tricorn has just announced that there'll be a big party in the Assembly Fields after the exam results this afternoon.

There's going to be a feast and music and the teachers are going to do a magic show!'

'Cool!' Troy exclaimed.

Willow grinned at him. 'Looks like we haven't missed all the fun stuff after all!'

As soon as lunch was over, the unicorns went to the Great Hall to get their exam results. Each desk had a name tag and a blank piece of paper on it. Willow's heart thudded as she found the desk with her name on. This was it! The moment they would find out how they had done. She glanced at Troy standing at the desk beside her.

'Good luck,' he whispered.

'You too,' replied Willow.

The Tricorn was waiting at the front of the hall. The chief elf stood beside him. As the last few unicorns found their desks, the Tricorn stamped his front left hoof on the ground. Absolute silence fell.

'It is now time for you to discover the results of your examinations,' the Tricorn told the waiting unicorns. 'When the horn is blown, you must touch your horn to the piece of paper in front of you. Count to three and, when you raise your heads, the paper will reveal your results.'

The chief elf raised the horn to his lips. The Tricorn nodded and a long note sounded. Taking a deep breath, Willow touched her horn to the paper. A small purple spark burst from the end of it. *One, two, three,* Willow counted, then raised her head. Purple writing had appeared.

<u>*Willow – Year One*</u>
<u>*Examination Results*</u>
Charms . . . Grade A (excellent)
Flying . . . Grade B (good)
Transformation . . . Grade B (good)
Weather Magic . . . Grade A (excellent)
Healing . . . Grade B (good)
History . . . Grade A (excellent)

Willow felt a *whoosh* of delight. She had passed all her exams and got a good or an excellent grade in every one! How amazing was that?

She swung round to find her friends. As she did so, the Tricorn's voice boomed out, 'When you have read your exam results, you may leave the hall.'

The unicorns immediately raced around the hall, all asking the same questions of their friends. 'What did you get? What grades?'

'Well?' Willow demanded as she, Storm, Sapphire and Troy met up. They were all smiling.

'I got As in transformation and weather magic and Bs in everything else, apart from flying, which I got a C in!' Storm burst out. 'But at least I passed it!'

'I got As in healing, weather magic and rose-quartz gazing, a B in charms and flying and a C in transformation,' said Sapphire, beaming.

Willow gabbled out her own results and then they all looked at Troy.

'I got an A in flying, healing, weather magic and charms,' he said slowly, 'a B in transformation. And in history . . .' He paused.

'Yes?' Willow demanded, hardly daring to breathe.

'I got a B!' Troy exclaimed. Willow, Sapphire and Storm whinnied in delight.

'You passed!' exclaimed Storm.

'You didn't just pass, you got a B!' said Sapphire.

'That's great, Troy!' Willow said.

Troy grinned round at them all. 'I couldn't have done it without your help. Thank you!' Willow didn't think she'd ever felt happier.

Oriel came over. 'Are you lot

coming to the party in the Assembly
Fields?' he asked.

Willow bucked joyfully. 'You bet!'
she said.

The end-of-term party was great
fun. There was a feast of fresh
shamrock and all sorts of games and
things to do – apple bobbing, a
lucky dip, pin the tail on the paper

unicorn, musical statues, flying races and guess the pixie's name. After the feast the teachers put on a magic show. Atlas and Fabian, the flying teachers, had everyone gasping as they flew four loop-the-loops one after the other, and on the final loop shot silver stars out of their horns. Tor turned a chair into a giant iced cake and made strings of mini unicorns to decorate the trees. Solaris, the weather magic teacher, made a glass of water change to ten different colours, first one after the other and then all together so the glass had multicoloured layers and looked like a rainbow. And the Tricorn demonstrated some of the most difficult unicorn magic by making himself invisible and reappearing behind trees and bushes in a silver flash. It was a brilliant display and at the end everyone cheered.

'This is just the best day ever!' said Willow happily.

As she spoke, an elf came over to Troy and gave him a piece of paper. 'It's a message from my parents,' Troy said, looking at the royal crown on the front. He opened it out and read what it said. 'Oh, wow! Listen to this:

Dear Troy,
Your mother and I have just heard
from the Tricorn about your excellent

exam results. We are delighted with how well you have done in your first year. Your mother tells me that in your last letter you asked if your friends Willow, Sapphire and Storm could come to stay with us at the palace for a week in the holidays. We would be delighted to have them come to visit . . .'

Willow, Storm and Sapphire gasped. Troy broke off and grinned at them. 'So, will you come to the palace?' he asked eagerly.

'Oh, yes!' they all whinnied.

Willow's mind raced. A trip to the palace and a chance to spend a whole week of the holidays with

Storm and Sapphire and Troy. It sounded brilliant!

'We'll be able to do loads of things,' Troy went on. 'There are sugar-coated apples growing on the trees, magic birds who sing whatever songs you want to hear, butterflies who perch on your back, and lots of secret passages in the castle to explore and play hide and seek in.'

'Wow!' said Sapphire.

'It'll be amazing,' said Willow.

'And best of all we'll be together,' Storm put in happily.

Willow grinned. 'No, what's really best of all is that after such a cool summer holiday we'll all be coming back here for another year!'

'And this time we'll be in Year Two,' Sapphire pointed out.

'I wonder what that will be like,' said Troy.

'One thing's for sure,' said Willow, tossing her mane excitedly. 'It's going to be fun!'